FERN HILL PRIMARY SCHOOL
RICHMOND ROAD
KINGSTON UPON THAMES
SURREY KT2 5PE
TELEPHONE: 020 8247 0300

FERN HILL PRIMARY SCHOOL
Richmond Road,
Kingston Upon Thames,
Surrey. KT2 5PE.
Telephone: 01

Text copyright © Roy Apps 1996
Illustrations copyright © Carla Daly 1996

First published in Great Britain in 1996
by Macdonald Young Books Ltd
Campus 400
Maylands Avenue
Hemel Hempstead
Herts HP2 7EZ

Designed and Typeset in Plantin by Backup... Design and Production, London.
Printed and bound in Belgium by Proost International Book Production.

British Library Cataloguing in Publication Data available.

ISBN: 0 7500 1913 1
ISBN: 0 7500 1914 X (pb)

ROY APPS

The Twitches' Bathday

Illustrated by Carla Daly

MACDONALD YOUNG BOOKS

CHAPTER ONE

It was dawn. The summer sun was only just beginning to glimmer through Gert and Lil's moth-eaten bedroom curtains.

Suddenly, a thin cracking sound, like an old ship's creaking timbers, filled the air. It was Gert's knees as she bent down to pull a copper cauldron full of icy water round to Lil's side of the bed.

Then there was a hissing sound, like a
slow puncture. It was Lil's breathing as she
struggled to drag a copper cauldron full of
icy water round to Gert's side of the bed.

Neither of them saw the other one, and
their bony bottoms backed nearer and
nearer to each other, until …

"Eeeikkk!!!"
shrieked Gert as she bumped backwards
into Lil.

"Aaargh!" howled Lil as she bumped backwards into Gert. She snorted when she saw the cauldron of icy water in Gert's hands. "Were you going to put that thing by my side of the bed so that I'd fall into it?"

"Course I was," cackled Gert. "It was meant to be a surpr-*ice* for you!" And she laughed long and loud at her very bad joke.

"Huh! I was really looking forward to seeing you leap out of bed into this!" croaked Lil. "After all, it is your bathday.*"

"It's your bathday too, you angel," snapped back Gert.

Now, it is hardly surprising that Gert and Lil shared the same bathday, because they

were *twitches*; that is, they were *twins* who were also *witches*. This year they were a hundred and fourteen years old.

*The Oxford Witchionary has this to say about Bathdays: *Bathday (n): A witch's birthday. The one day in the year when witches are supposed to have a bath. But having a bath, even just once a year, is once too often for a witch.*

"No one else had better try to give us a bath," threatened Gert, "otherwise I'll curse them!"

"I can't see that they will; no one else knows it's our bathday, do they, bat brain?" snapped back Lil.

"No I don't suppose they –"

Gert was cut off in mid-sentence by a thunderous knock on the front door.

"Now I wonder who that can be," frowned Lil, edging towards the door.

"No Lil! Don't go! It might be someone come to give us a bath!" trembled Gert.

Lil stopped in her tracks. "You're right," she agreed. With a look of horror on both their craggy old faces, the twitches dived under their moulding duvet.

But the thunderous knocking continued. From the bottom of the bed, Lil spat out a mouthful of old toenail clippings.

"There's nothing else for it Gert, we'll just have to go down and face the intruders, whoever they are," she declared.

And so, with their knobbly knees knocking nervously like castanets, Gert and Lil made their way down the stairs to the front door …

CHAPTER TWO

Gert undid the rusty chains and Lil slid
back the squeaky bolts on the front door.
They peered out and came face to face
with Nosey Jose, the local postman.

"I couldn't get this in your letter box," he
said, "it's all bunged up."

"We've got a family of cockroaches
nesting there," explained Lil.

Nosey Jose stuffed a large letter into Gert's hand and quickly backed away up the path.

"Come on," snapped Lil, dragging Gert back indoors. "What's in that letter then? Nobody ever sends us letters."

Gert opened the letter and stared hard at it with her beady eyes. "It's not a *letter*," she exclaimed. "It's a *telegram*!"

"Let's see then, you angel!" snapped Lil, grabbing the telegram from her sister.

She tore it open. This is what it said:

Dear Gertrude and Lily

*Happy Birthday – or should I say
Bathday! Sorry this is 14 years late, but I'm
only just getting the hang of my
computerised birthday telegram list.*

Yours Royally,

E Regina – (ie. the Queen)

"Why has the Queen written to *us*?" asked Gert in a puzzled voice.

"Didn't you know? She sends everyone a telegram on their hundredth birthday," explained Lil with a superior kind of sniff.

Gert shivered and poked a grubby finger at the Queen's telegram. "I don't like it. I don't like it one bit. And the one bit I especially don't like is that bit," she frowned, "about her *computerised birthday telegram list*. Supposing someone hacked into it?"

"You're right." Lil winced. "Everyone would get to know when our bathday was and they'd all be banging on our front door, trying to give us a wash. It doesn't bear thinking about."

"We've got to get our names removed from that computer mailing list at once!" said Gert. "And there's only way to do that: we'll have to go to London to see the Queen!"

"Good idea," said Lil. "We'll take her a small present, just to show her what loyal subjects we are."

And she picked up a bottle of Eau de
Crone from the hall table.*

---

*Eau de Crone is a special twitch's perfume made
from bad eggs and rotten Brussels sprouts, which are
spiced with Parmesan cheese and soaked for thirteen days
in a dirty old sock full of scummy drain water.*

CHAPTER THREE

"You don't think anyone here knows it's our bathday do you?" Gert asked Lil nervously as they got off the train in London.

"Don't be a nit-witty natterjack all your life," snarled her sister.

They passed a guard about to wave off another train.

"Are you ladies going to Bath?" he asked, with a smile.

"I told you, you angel!" screeched Gert. "He knows it's our bathday!" She and Lil raced off out of the station as fast as their spindly legs would carry them. So fast, in fact, that they didn't see the sign saying:

THIS TRAIN FOR BATH, BRISTOL AND CARDIFF

As Gert and Lil approached the Palace gates, they saw queues of people; the men all dressed in smart suits and top hats and the ladies in silky, summery dresses.

"Look!" hissed Gert.

"It's only a queue of people," snapped Lil.

"Yes, but look where they're standing!"

Lil squinted hard and saw that they were all standing by an enormous fountain.

"Do you know what they're waiting for?"
Lil shook her head.

"The Queen's told them all it's our
bathday," reasoned Gert. "They're waiting
to chuck us into that fountain."

"Curse them all!" muttered Lil.

"Good idea!" agreed Gert. She and Lil leapt out of the shadows and began dancing round the crowd of people.

"Snakes and toads and huge rats' tails
Spiders and ants and lice
Whoever receives this fearsome curse –

"Oi! You two!" a voice suddenly boomed from behind them.

Gert and Lil spun round to find themselves face-to-face with the end of a bayonet. Holding the bayonet was a guardsman in a furry hat. He was a great tower of a man with eyes like gobstoppers and teeth like bullets.

"You're under arrest!" he bawled. Gert
and Lil didn't bother to argue. They threw
their hands up into the air, while the
guardsman searched their pockets.

Which is when he found Lil's bottle of
Eau de Crone. He began to unscrew the top.

"Careful! That's very expensive and fine
perfume that is!" protested Lil.

But the top was already off. The
guardsman sniffed. Hard.

"Caw! Eurgh! Pooh!" he spat, "it's putrid!" He clutched his stomach and his face began to turn a sickly shade of green. "Ooer, I think I'm going to be sick!"

"Quick!" yelled Lil. And before the guardsman had time to recover, she and Gert had skipped over his bayonet, leapt over the wrought iron gates and dashed through the front door of Buckingham Palace.

CHAPTER FOUR

Gert and Lil crept along the long, carpeted corridors of Buckingham Palace. Suddenly, they heard a distant rustle and swish; then the faint sound of someone whistling. As they stood there, Gert and Lil realised that the rustling, swishing and whistling were getting closer.

"Quick, in here," whispered Lil.

Gert and Lil dived through a half open door.

"Aargh!" screeched Lil.

"Eeiikkk!" screamed Gert.

And no wonder, for they were in the Queen's bathroom.

No sooner had the horror of their situation sunk in, than Gert and Lil saw the door open.

In swished a regal lady wearing a crown
and a floral bath robe. It was the Queen.

"Oh!" she said, in a mildly-surprised
kind of voice. "Umm … are you guests, or
servants?"

"We're *twitches*," said Lil. "and if you don't take our names of your computerised birthday telegram list, we'll turn you into a warty toad."

"Yes! So *there*!" added Gert.

But the Queen didn't look at all worried. "Warty toads have it easy. They never have to bath," she sighed.

Gert and Lil couldn't believe their ears. "Er … don't you like having a bath, either?" asked Gert.

"One finds them tiresome, time-consuming and very wet," said the Queen. "And when one is a Queen, one is expected to bath at least three times a day. But let's get to the point; just what are you doing in my bathroom?"

Gert and Lil explained all about witches bathdays, and how they were afraid that someone would try and give them a bath.

"So, you'd like your names removed from one's birthday mailing list?"

Gert and Lil nodded.

"And you say you're twitches?"

Gert and Lil nodded again.

"I think that can be arranged ..."

Gert and Lil beamed toothy grins.

"...but in return you must do something for me."

"What's that, your Maj?" asked Gert.

"One has a garden party in the grounds this afternoon – that's why I've got to have yet another bath. One finds these occasions *so boring*. I'd like you to do a few tricks and a bit of magic to enliven the proceedings."

Lil shook her head. "We're retired twitches. We don't do tricks any more ..."

"Do you want your names removed from my birthday list or not?" asked the Queen, stiffly.

"You don't understand your Maj. None of our magic seems to work these days," explained Gert. "Not even the curses."

But the Queen's face was set firm. And it's no good arguing with a Queen whose face is set firm.

Gert and Lil sighed a crabby sigh. "Very well. Your wish is our command, your Maj."

CHAPTER FIVE

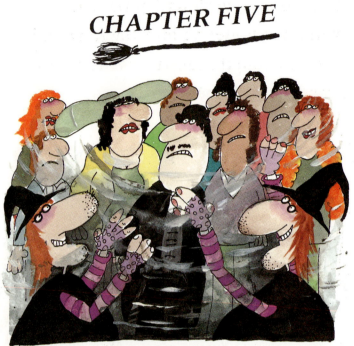

Gert and Lil danced wildly in front of the Buckingham Palace garden party guests and chanted:

"Snakes and toads and huge rats' tails
Spiders and ants and lice
Whoever receives this fearsome curse
Might find something happening to them
that isn't very nice
Er … perhaps"

But of course, nothing happened. Everyone was fidgeting and yawning and looking very bored indeed. Everyone, that is, except the Queen, who was looking crossly at Gert and Lil.

"There are two hundred and fifty garden party guests out there," she said. "Do you want me to tell them that it's your bathday today? I'm sure they'd all be only too willing to lend a hand with the scrubbing brush."

Gert and Lil shivered in their boots. "No not that!" pleaded Lil.

"I've already alerted Torquil my Chief Footman to the possibility," said the Queen. Out the corner of their eyes, Gert and Lil spotted the Palace Footman with a large bar of soap in each hand and a towel across each arm. "You wouldn't ... would you your Maj?" Gert's tone was desperate.

"I might if you don't start doing some tricks soon. And quickly!" muttered the Queen darkly.

"But it's no use, your Maj," sighed Gert.

"You were never any use," Lil taunted her sister.

"Useless yourself, crab-face!" snapped Gert. She stood back to give her sister a good thump, swung her fist round and knocked Lil's hat clean off her head. There was a slight stirring movement in Lil's hair, then out slid a spider's web as big as a hairnet.

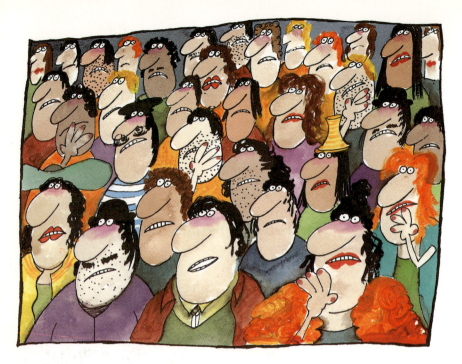

Everyone gasped in excited surprise, but
neither Gert nor Lil noticed, because Lil
was busy pulling roughly at Gert's sleeve.
As she did so, a puff of ancient dust rose
into the air and a startled bat flew out of
her armpit.

"Bravo! Bravo!" shouted the Queen, but
Gert and Lil didn't hear. They were still
arguing. As Lil stamped on Gert's toes, a
huge newt sprang out of the top of her boot.

39

The garden party guests all clapped and cheered and agreed that watching Gert and Lil's tricks was even better than seeing a

conjuror saw a lady in half. "Torquil!" called the Queen to her Chief Footman, who was also her Chief Computer Programmer. "Remove the twitches' names from my birthday card list at once!"

The Queen turned to Gert and Lil. "This has turned into one's best garden party ever," she said. "Do help yourselves to cucumber sandwiches."

"If it's all the same with you, your Maj," said Gert, "cucumber sandwiches aren't really to our taste."

"Oh dear," frowned the Queen. Then her face brightened. "I've got something you'd like. Just dip your fingers in the bowl marked Royal Jelly."

Into the bowl marked Royal Jelly went
Gert and Lil's fingers.

"It's … lightly grilled frog's spawn!"
exclaimed Lil, in a voice so loud a number
of the guests heard and began to look a bit
faint.

"Shhhh!" said the Queen, "one mustn't
upset one's guests. Lightly grilled frog's
spawn has been a favourite dish of mine

ever since I first visited the Inner Outer
Pollywallidoodle Islands in 1947."

"It's our favourite, too!" beamed Gert,
tucking in.

CHAPTER SIX

As they opened the front door of their hovel that evening, Gert said, "What a really grotty bathday," which is a witch's way of saying a most excellent time has been had by all.

Lil agreed. "Yes, but I am tired," she yawned. "I think I'll go straight to bed."

"Me too," said Gert.

As they climbed the stairs, Gert said, "To think, now that the Queen's taken us off her mailing list, no one will ever know when it's our bathday."

"No, we'll never ever have to have a bath for the rest of our lives," mused Lil, smiling broadly.

They opened the bedroom door. Gert walked round to her side of the big, buggy bed. Lil walked round to her side of the big, buggy bed. Suddenly they remembered what they'd each left there that morning –

But too late.

SPL-A-A-ASH!!!!

"Oh no- a-a-a-a-a-rgh!" screamed Gert.

"Oh no e-e-e-ikkk!" screeched Lil.

HAPPY BATHDAY TWITCHES!

Look out for more gruesomely funny titles in the Red Storybook series:

The Twitches by Roy Apps

Gert and Lil are fed up. Although they've been witching for 113 years, they've never made up a successful magic spell. Something drastic needs to be done ...

The Twitches on Horriday by Roy Apps

"Witches don't have holidays," Gert Explained. "They have horridays!" When Gert and Lil win a free trip to Spain, the posh hotel is a terrible disappointment – there are no cobwebs in sight, the restaurant won't serve warty toads, and the rooms smell as if they've been cleaned ... urgh!

The Twitches' Chrissy-Mess by Roy Apps

It's Christmas Eve, and Gert and Lil are putting up their Chrissy-Mess decorations. There are spiders' webs, snail's slime, and a plate of mice pies and freshly squeezed beetle juice for Father Christmas. It's bound to be a cackling good Chrissy-Mess for all.

Wonderwitch by Helen Muir

Wonderwitch has all a witch could want – a tall hat, a black cat and a broomstick. But she's bored with turning people into toads, and decides to try something different ...

Storybooks are available from your local bookshop or can be ordered direct from the publishers. For more information about Storybooks, write to: *The Sales Department, Macdonald Young Books, Maylands Avenue, Hemel Hempstead, Herts HP2 7EZ.*